Silly Bunny Tales

Grosset & Dunlap
An Imprint of Penguin Group (USA) Inc.

GROSSET & DUNLAP
Published by the Penguin Group
Penguin Group (USA) Inc., 375 Hudson Street, New York, New York 10014, USA
Penguin Group (Canada), 90 Eglinton Avenue East, Suite 700,
Toronto, Ontario M4P 2Y3, Canada
(a division of Pearson Penguin Canada Inc.)
Penguin Books Ltd., 80 Strand, London WC2R 0RL, England
Penguin Group Ireland, 25 St. Stephen's Green, Dublin 2, Ireland
(a division of Penguin Books Ltd.)
Penguin Group (Australia), 250 Camberwell Road, Camberwell, Victoria 3124, Australia
(a division of Pearson Australia Group Pty. Ltd.)
Penguin Books India Pvt. Ltd., 11 Community Centre, Panchsheel Park,
New Delhi—110 017, India
Penguin Group (NZ), 67 Apollo Drive, Rosedale, Auckland 0632, New Zealand
(a division of Pearson New Zealand Ltd.)
Penguin Books (South Africa) (Pty.) Ltd., 24 Sturdee Avenue,
Rosebank, Johannesburg 2196, South Africa

Penguin Books Ltd., Registered Offices:
80 Strand, London WC2R 0RL, England

Based upon the animated series *Max & Ruby*
A Nelvana Limited production © 2002–2003.

Max & Ruby © Rosemary Wells. Licensed by Nelvana Limited. NELVANA is a registered trademark of Nelvana Limited. CORUS is a trademark
of Corus Entertainment Inc. All rights reserved. Published in 2013 by Grosset & Dunlap, a division of Penguin Young Readers Group,
345 Hudson Street, New York, New York 10014. GROSSET & DUNLAP is a trademark of Penguin Group (USA) Inc. Manufactured in China.

ISBN 978-0-448-46308-7   10 9 8 7 6 5 4 3 2 1

 ALWAYS LEARNING   **PEARSON**

Picture Perfect

Ruby and Max went to Rosalinda's gift shop to get
a birthday present for Grandma.
Ruby chose a beautiful locket.

"I bet Grandma would love to have a picture of you and Max in her locket," said Rosalinda. "Why don't you try out our new photo booth? It's only a quarter for four pictures." "Perfect!" said Ruby.

But Max wasn't interested. He wanted a pair of glasses with a nose and mustache.

"Max, please take off those silly glasses," said Ruby. "We need to take a nice picture for Grandma's locket."

Max put the glasses, nose, and mustache in his pocket.

Ruby took Max into the photo booth.

Ruby put a quarter in the slot.
"Sit very still, Max," said Ruby. "We have four chances to take the perfect picture."

Ruby pushed the camera button.
"Smile at the camera, Max," said Ruby.
But Max forgot to smile.

"Oh no," said Ruby. "These pictures are no good.
We'll have to try again."

Ruby pushed the button again.
"Smile this time, Max," said Ruby.

But Max smiled too late.
"These pictures are even worse!" said Ruby.

"Third time's a charm, Max!" said Ruby.
But Max had a better idea. He pulled out his vampire teeth.

"Max," said Ruby. "Grandma doesn't like vampires!
Let's try again."

In the photo booth, Max tried to put on the glasses,
nose, and mustache. Ruby took them from him, but the
camera flashed before she could put them away.

"Oh no, Max," said Ruby. "Our last set of pictures is ruined!"

But Grandma didn't think the picture in her locket was ruined.

She loved it. Glasses, nose, mustache, and all!

It was a rainy day.
"Let's draw a puzzle to play with Grandma when she comes to visit, Max," said Ruby.

"Trains!" said Max.

"Max," said Ruby. "I think Grandma likes puzzles better than trains."

"I'm going to draw an amazing maze," said Ruby.
"Choo-choo!" said Max.

Ruby took out her markers and a drawing pad. She started to draw squiggly paths with a yellow marker. But Max had an idea.

"Choo-choo!" said Max.

Max had taken Ruby's other markers. He was making pretend trees for his train to pass.

"Forest!" said Max.

"Max, I need my markers back. But that's a good idea for what to draw—trees!" said Ruby.

Ruby drew trees all over her maze.
"I'm thirsty, Max," said Ruby. "Let's have blueberry juice!"
"Choo-choo!" said Max.

Ruby came back with blueberry juice. Meanwhile, Max had used her drawing pad to make a bridge for his train. "Max, I need my drawing pad back. But that's a good idea for what to draw—bridges!" said Ruby.

Ruby drew five bridges over the roads in her maze.

"Choo-choo! Choo-choo!" said Max as he revved up his train engine.

BAM! Max's train went right into Ruby's glass of juice. The juice made a blueberry lake on her maze and spilled on the rug.

"Uh-oh!" said Ruby. Just then, the doorbell rang. "Max, why don't you let Grandma in while I clean this up."

"Hello, Max," said Grandma. "What are you doing on this rainy day?"

"Playing trains!" said Max.

"I love trains!" said Grandma.

"And I made a maze for you!" said Ruby.
"What an interesting maze, Ruby!" said Grandma.
"The lake is beautiful. It's just the right color!"

"Lake Blueberry!" said Ruby and Max.

It was the hottest day of the summer.
Ruby and Louise were making an art stand to sell
their paintings.

Max wanted to help.
"Max," said Ruby. "The best thing you can do is find a place to cool off."

Max found a fan on the windowsill.
"Ah, cool!" said Max.

"Max," said Ruby. "You shouldn't be near fans, and the air is blowing all our paintings away. Can you find another way to cool down?"

Max turned on the garden sprinkler.

"Ah, cool!" said Max.
But the water was getting Ruby's and Louise's paintings wet.
"Max, can you find a less wet way to cool down?" said Ruby.

Max went inside and got an ice pop from the fridge.
"Ah, cool!" said Max.

But the ice pop dripped on the paintings.
"Max, can you find a less messy way to cool down?"
said Ruby.

"Actually," said Louise, "ice pops sound good. How about we get some for ourselves? We don't have any customers, anyway."

"Good idea, Louise," said Ruby. "Max, can you watch the art stand for us?"

Max watched the stand. But it was very, very hot on the sidewalk. Soon he had a better idea.

Ruby and Louise came back with ice pops.
"Max, what did you do?" said Ruby. "You weren't
supposed to use my art to make a sun hat!"

Just then, a customer arrived. And she wanted . . . one of Max's sun hats! And another one for her little bunny!

"Cool!" said Max.